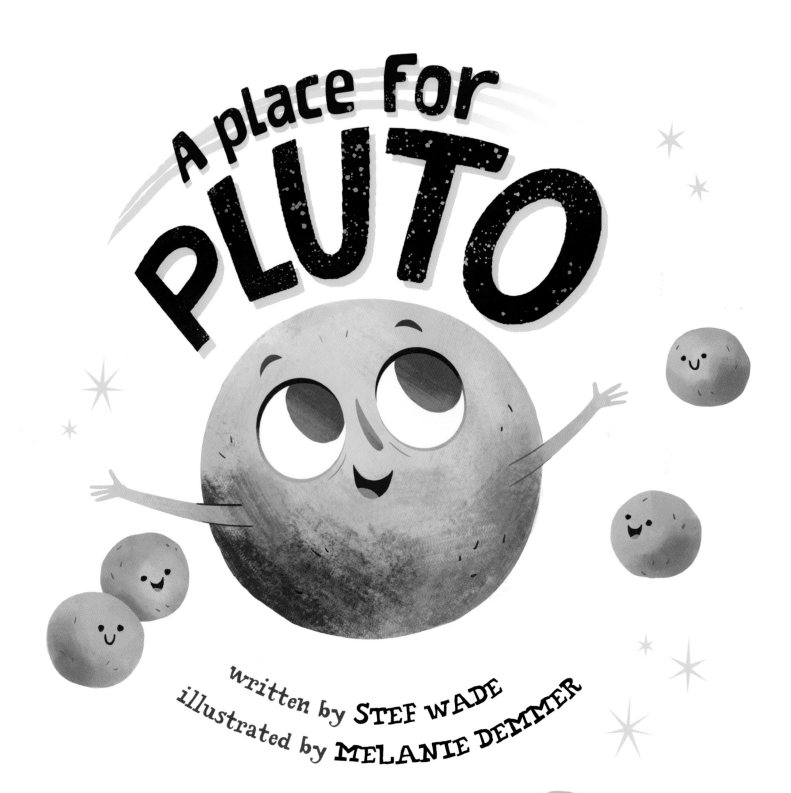

A place for PLUTO

written by STEF WADE
illustrated by MELANIE DEMMER

CAPSTONE EDITIONS
a capstone imprint

A Place For Pluto is published by
Capstone Editions, a Capstone imprint
1710 Roe Crest Drive
North Mankato, Minnesota 56003
www.mycapstone.com

Library of Congress Cataloging-in-Publication data
will be available on the Library of Congress website.

ISBN: 978-1-68446-004-5 (hardcover)
ISBN: 978-1-68446-005-2 (ebook)

Designer: Aruna Rangarajan

Printed and bound in China.
306

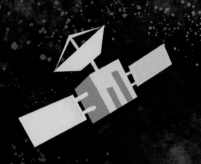

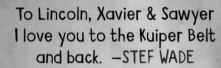

To Lincoln, Xavier & Sawyer
I love you to the Kuiper Belt
and back. —STEF WADE

To my parents, whose support
for me is out of this world.
—MELANIE DEMMER

For the better part of forever, Pluto was a planet. One of the

FAMOUS NINE.

He was the smallest and the farthest from the sun, but he was proud just the same.

Even though Pluto orbited around the sun and was mostly round, the creatures on Earth decided he was

TOO SMALL.

Pluto was
CRUSHED.

He tried to
PROTEST.

#PLUTOBELONGS

NOT

FAIR

STAND

WITH

PLUTO

But it was **NO USE.**

There,
there.

Feeling sad and rejected, Pluto left with Charon and his other four moons by his side to find his place in the galaxy.

As Pluto moved along, his friend
Halley's Comet streaked past.

Haven't seen
you in awhile!

Pluto wasn't a comet or a planet.
HE WAS A NOBODY.

Feeling more blue than brown,
Pluto kept moving.

When Pluto saw Gem, Persi, and Ori crashing in as dusty, rocky comet tails, he wondered if he could join them.

Then Ida the asteroid orbited by. Pluto and Ida were nearly the same size. Pluto thought he'd finally figured out his true identity.

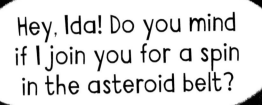

Pluto wasn't a planet
or a comet or an asteroid.
He missed being a planet.
He missed his old friends.

HE MISSED FEELING LIKE HE BELONGED.

No one in the solar system
was a match for Pluto.

He spun around the sun like
everyone else, but he wasn't
a planet or a comet or an
asteroid or a meteoroid.

Pluto had nowhere to turn. He was about to give up when he saw someone he'd never seen before. He felt like he was

LOOKING IN A MIRROR!

Pardon me if I sound rude, but what are you?

Pluto stared in wonder at the four dwarf planets. They were too small to be planets but too big to be rocks. They were not planets or comets or asteroids or meteoroids. They were

JUST LIKE HIM!

Pluto felt more like himself than ever before. He couldn't wait to tell his old friends about his new ones. Turns out his old friends missed him too!

WHAT'S THE DEAL WITH PLUTO?

In 1930, Pluto was discovered as the ninth planet in the solar system.

I made it! Awesome!

In 2006, Pluto was told he was not a planet anymore.

Bummer.

POOR PLUTO! WHY?

Scientists decided that to be a planet, it must

- orbit around the sun. ✓

- have a round shape. ✓

- be able to clear its own orbit by pulling asteroids toward itself, making the asteroids part of the planet.

Are you kidding me with this?

Pluto does orbit around the sun and is mostly round. But Pluto is small (only half the size of the United States) and shares the area around its orbit with Neptune and many other large objects in an area called the Kuiper Belt.

BFFs!

But Pluto isn't alone. Other dwarf planets like Ceres, Eris, Haumea, and Makemake cannot clear an object out of their paths either.